One Morning in Maine

One Morning in Maine

BY ROBERT McCLOSKEY

Puffin Books

PUFFIN BOOKS
Published by the Penguin Group
Penguin Putnam Books for Young Readers, 345 Hudson Street,
New York, New York 10014, U.S.A.
Penguin Books Ltd, 27 Wrights Lane, London W8 5TZ, England
Penguin Books Australia Ltd, Ringwood, Victoria, Australia
Penguin Books Canada Ltd, 10 Alcorn Avenue, Toronto, Ontario, Canada M4V 3B2
Penguin Books (N.Z.) Ltd, 182-190 Wairau Road, Auckland 10, New Zealand

Penguin Books Ltd, Registered Offices: Harmondsworth, Middlesex, England

First published by The Viking Press 1952
Viking Seafarer Edition published 1971
Reprinted 1972, 1974
Published in Picture Puffins 1976

40   39

ISBN 0 14 050.174 6
Library of Congress catalog card number: 52-6983

Printed in Mexico.
Set in Foundry Goudy Modern

One morning in Maine, Sal woke up. She peeked over the top of the covers. The bright sunlight made her blink, so she pulled the covers up and was just about to go back to sleep when she remembered "today is the day I am going to Buck's Harbor with my father!"

Sal pushed back the covers, hopped out of bed, put on her robe and slippers, and hurried out into the hall.

There was little Jane, just coming out of her room. Sister Jane had wiggled out of her nightie, so Sal helped her put on her robe and slippers. "You don't want to catch cold and have to stay in bed, Jane, because this morning we are going to Buck's Harbor," Sal reminded her sister.

Together they went into the bathroom to get ready for
breakfast. Sal squeezed out toothpaste on sister Jane's brush
and said, "Be careful, Jane, and don't get it in your hair."

Then she squeezed some toothpaste on her own brush and

when she started to brush her teeth something felt *very strange! One of her teeth felt loose!* She wiggled it with her tongue, then she wiggled it with her finger.

"Oh, dear!" thought Sal. "This *cannot* be true!"

Standing on the stool, she looked in the mirror and wiggled her tooth again. Sure enough, it was loose! You could even *see* it wiggle.

"Ma-a-a-ma!" she cried. "One of my teeth is loose! It will hurt and I'll have to stay in bed! I won't be able to eat my breakfast and go with Daddy to Buck's Harbor!" She came running down the stairs and into the kitchen.

"Why, Sal," said her mother, "that's nothing to worry about. That means that today you've become a big girl. Everybody's baby teeth get loose and come out when they grow up. A nice new bigger and better tooth will grow in when this one comes out."

"Did your baby teeth get loose and come out when you grew to be a big girl?" Sal asked her mother.

"Yes," she answered. "And then these nice large ones grew in. When Penny grew to be a big dog, his puppy teeth dropped out too."

"And will Jane's get loose too?" asked Sal.

"Yes," said her mother. "But not for a long time, not until she stops being a baby and grows up to be a big girl like you. Jane is so young that she hasn't even grown all her baby teeth yet. Now let's all go upstairs and brush our hair and get dressed for breakfast."

"It feels so different to be a big girl and have a loose tooth," said Sal, "especially when you are chewing. When is it going to come out?"

"Perhaps today, perhaps tomorrow," answered her mother. "But when your tooth does come out, you put it under your pillow and make a wish, and your wish is supposed to come true."

"I know what I'm going to wish for!" said Sal. "A nice cold choco—"

"But you mustn't tell anybody your wish, or it won't come true," cautioned her mother. "It's supposed to be a *secret* wish. Now finish your milk, Sal; then you can go out on the beach and help your father dig clams for lunch."

"I'm a big girl, and I can help him dig a lot of clams, fast," said Sal, "so we can hurry up and go to Buck's Harbor."

After breakfast, when Sal went out to help her father, she saw a fish hawk flying overhead, carrying a fish.

"I have a loose tooth!" Sal called up to the fish hawk. The fish hawk flew straight to her nest on top of a tree without answering. She was too busy feeding breakfast to her baby fish hawk.

Sal wondered for a moment if the baby fish hawk had any teeth to chew his breakfast. Then she started on down toward the beach where her father was digging clams.

When she came near to the water she saw a loon.

"I have a loose tooth!" Sal called to the loon. "And today I have started to be a big girl."

The loon didn't say anything but kept swimming in circles. Then he ducked his beak in the water and snapped out a herring. Then he swallowed it *whole*, without a single chew.

"Perhaps loons don't have teeth," thought Sal, and she was just turning to go on her way

when a seal poked his head up out of the water.

"I have a loose tooth!" Sal said to the seal, and the seal, being just as curious as most seals, swam nearer to have a good look.

"See?" said Sal, and she walked closer, right down onto the slippery seaweeds at the water's edge.

The seal swam nearer, and Sal was stooping nearer when

O-O-Oops! she slipped on the seaweed and fell kasploosh!

The seal disappeared beneath the water and the loon laughed, "Luh-hoo-hoo-hoo-hoo-hooh!"

Sal wasn't hurt a bit, so she laughed too, then she got up carefully

and started on down the shore to help her father dig clams.

She paused to watch some sea gulls having breakfast. They were dropping mussels down on a rock to crack the mussel shells, just like nuts. Then they flew down to eat the insides.

"Do sea gulls have teeth?" wondered Sal as she wiggled her own loose one with her tongue. She thought of her secret wish and smiled, then hurried down the beach to where she could see her father.

"Daddy! I have a loose tooth!" she shouted. "And when it drops out I'm going to put it under my pillow and wish a wish. You can even see it wiggle!"

Her father stopped digging clams to watch while Sal wiggled her tooth for him. "You're growing into a big girl when you get a loose tooth!" he said. "What are you going to wish for when it drops out?"

"I can't tell you that," said Sal solemnly, "because it's supposed to be a *secret* wish."

"Oh, yes, so it is," her father agreed.

"May I help you dig clams?" Sal asked.

"I'm almost finished," he replied, "but you can help if you like. First, you must take off your shoes and socks, and roll up your pants too, so that they won't get all wet and muddy."

Sal took off her shoes and socks and put them on a dry rock. She rolled up her pants and waded into the muddy gravel to help her father. He dug in the mud with his clam rake, and then they looked carefully and felt around in the muddy hole for clams.

"I found a tiny baby one!" said Sal.

"You certainly did," said her father. "But it's too small. We just keep the large ones, like this. Let's put the baby clam back in the mud so he can grow to be a big clam some day."

"He *is* such a baby clam, and I guess he *is* too small," she agreed.

"I guess he isn't even big enough to have all his baby teeth," said Sal, placing the tiny clam tenderly back in the mud.

"Clams don't have teeth," grunted her father, digging another rakeful of mud.

"Not even big clams have teeth?" asked Sal.

"Not even big clams," her father assured her.

"Do baby fish hawks and big fish hawks have teeth?" asked Sal.

"No," said her father.

"Do loons have teeth?" she asked, "and gulls?"

"No."

"Do seals have teeth?"

"Yes, they have 'em," he answered.

"And do their teeth get loose like this?" asked Sal, opening her mouth to show her loose tooth.

"O-owh!" she said with great surprise. She felt with her tongue, and she felt with her muddy fingers.

"Why it's *gone!*" she said sadly, feeling once more just to make sure. The loose tooth was really and truly gone. The salty mud from her fingers tasted bitter, and she made a bitter-tasting face that was almost a face like crying.

"Did you swallow it, Sal?" her father asked with a concerned smile.

"No." She shook her head sadly. "I was too busy asking to do any swallowing. It just dropped itself out. It's gone, and I can't put it under my pillow and make my wish come true!"

"That's too bad," her father sympathized. "But you are growing into a big girl, and big girls don't cry about a little thing like that. They wait for another tooth to come loose and make a wish on that one."

"Maybe we can find my tooth where it dropped," said Sal, hopefully feeling around in the muddy gravel where the clams live.

Sal's father helped her look, but a muddy tooth looks so much like a muddy pebble, and a muddy pebble looks so much like a muddy tooth, that they hunted and hunted without finding it.

"We'll have to stop looking and take our clams back to the house, Sal," her father said at last, "or we won't have time for the trip to the village." He washed off the clams in the clean salt water of the bay, and Sal reluctantly stopped looking and waded in to wash the mud from her feet and hands.

"I guess some clam will find my tooth and get what I wished for," said Sal. "If we come back here tomorrow and find a clam eating a chocolate ice-cream cone, why, we'll have to take it away from him and make him give my tooth back too," she said.

39

While Sal put on her socks and shoes her father packed seaweed around the clams to keep them moist and fresh.

"Now, let's hurry back to the house," he said, "and in a few minutes we'll be on our way to Buck's Harbor in the boat to get milk and groceries."

"Okay," Sal answered, scrambling to her feet.

She gave one last look at the muddy place where she'd lost her tooth and then started walking back along the shore with her father. She walked along slowly, looking at her feet so that her father could not see her face, in case it looked almost like crying.

"Oh! See what I've found!" she exclaimed, stooping to pick up a feather.

"It's a gull's feather," said her father, pausing for Sal to pick it up.

"Did a gull lose it? Will another feather grow in where this one dropped out?" asked Sal.

"Yes, Sal, that's right," answered her father.

"Maybe sea gulls put dropped-out feathers under their pillows and wish secret wishes," Sal suggested.

"Sea gulls don't use pillows, but I suppose they can make wishes," her father said.

"Then I'll make my wish on this *feather*," Sal decided.

"Perhaps the sea gull has already made a wish on that feather and the wish is used up," suggested her father.

"Oh, no," Sal said definitely, "he didn't, you see. I guess because he was too busy flying and not looking back. He didn't notice it was loose when he brushed his feathers this morning, so he didn't expect it would drop out. He doesn't even know it's gone," she convinced herself. She closed her eyes tight and wished her secret wish.

When they reached home Sal's mother and sister Jane were waiting with a box of empty milk bottles to return to the store and a list of things to buy.

"I'll have a nice clam chowder ready for your lunch when you get back," said Sal's mother, waving good-by.

"I'll take good care of Jane," Sal promised. "I'm a big girl and I can watch so she doesn't tumble into the water."

Sal and Jane and their father went down to the shore and got aboard their boat.

Sal and Jane put on their life preservers while their father prepared to start the outboard motor. He pulled and he pulled on the rope to start it, but the outboard motor just coughed and sputtered and wouldn't start.

So he had to row the boat all the way across the bay to Buck's Harbor where the store was.

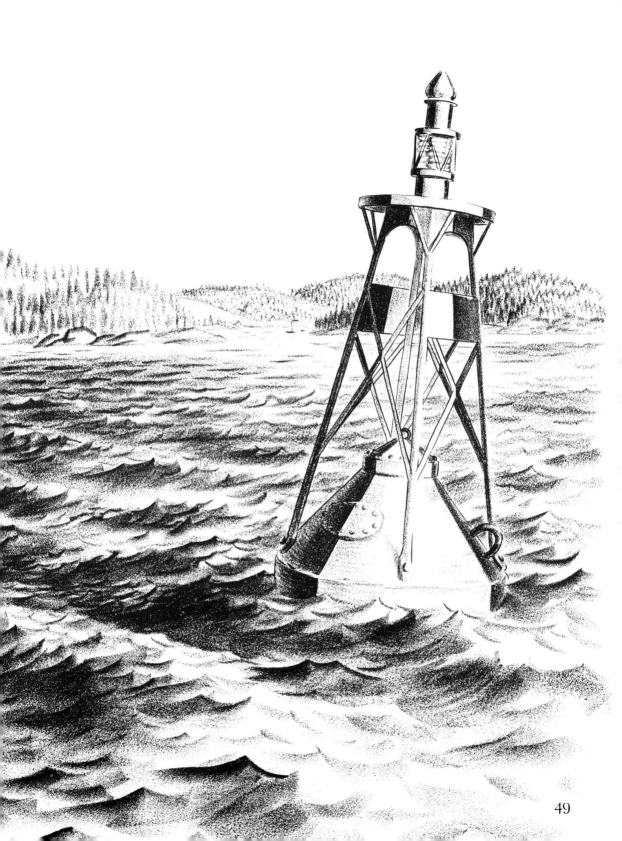

The harbor was full of boats, and Sal's father rowed their boat among them, up to a landing, and tied it so it would not drift away while they were at the store. They all climbed ashore, and Sal's father brought along the milk bottles. He brought the outboard motor too, so Mr. Condon who ran the garage could fix it.

As they came up the path to the village Mr. Condon was outside his garage, putting gas into a car.

"I have a tooth out!" Sal greeted. "And our outboard motor won't run."

"My, such trouble!" Mr. Condon commented, and after he had admired the empty place where Sal's tooth was missing

they took the outboard motor into the garage to find why it wouldn't run. Mr. Condon pinched a little with his pliers, tunked a bit with his hammer, and then, after selecting a large wrench, he took out the spark plug.

"Came right out, just like that tooth of yours, didn't it, Sal?" he said, holding it up to the light. "Humph!" he grunted, tossing it on the floor. "Needs a new plug!"

Sal was just about to ask how long it would take for a new spark plug to grow in when Mr. Condon reached up on the shelf

and picked out a brand-new one, and put it in the motor.

Sal picked up the old spark plug and handed it to sister Jane. Jane was so little that she didn't understand about secret wishes. Jane was so little that she couldn't even say ice-cream cone! So Sal wished the secret wish for Jane on the spark plug.

Mr. Condon pulled the rope, and the motor started right up, just as good as new. Sal's father thanked him and picked

54

up the motor and the milk bottles. Jane carried her spark plug, Sal carried her feather, and they said good-by and walked across the street to where Mr. Condon's brother kept store.

56

"Well, look who's here!" said the Mr. Condon who kept store.

"I have a tooth out!" Sal shouted, returning Mr. Condon's greeting.

She showed the empty place where her tooth had been, first to Mr. Condon, then to Mr. Ferd Clifford and Mr. Oscar Staples, who were sitting in the store talking about trapping lobsters and how the fish were biting.

"Don't put your tongue in the empty place," Mr. Clifford advised, "and a nice shiny gold one like mine will grow in."

"But I didn't know soon enough," said Sal, looking confused.

"Hawh!" said Mr. Condon, chuckling. "Don't you go worry-in' about everything these jokers suggest. I don't suppose," he added, opening up his freezer, "that you could eat an ice-cream cone with one of your teeth out?"

"Oh, yes, I could!" said Sal. "And it's supposed to be chocolate!"

"And this little lady?" he questioned, turning to Jane.

"Hers is supposed to be vanilla, so the drips won't spot, and you'd better push it together tight, so it won't drop off," Sal dictated, "because she's still almost a baby and doesn't even have all of her first teeth."

After Mr. Condon had put the groceries and milk in the box, they thanked him once more and waved good-by. They walked down the path to the harbor

and down the runway to the float where their boat was tied. They all climbed aboard, carrying the outboard motor, the box of milk and groceries, the feather, the spark plug, and the ice-cream cones.

While their father fastened the outboard motor to the boat Sal and Jane finished their ice-cream cones.

"I want s'more!" Jane demanded.

"Silly!" exclaimed Sal. "Our wishes are all used up." Then she remembered that she was growing up, and just like a grownup she said, "Besides, Jane, two ice-cream cones would ruin your appetite. When we get home we're going to have

CLAM CHOWDER FOR LUNCH!"